This book belongs to:

A catalogue record for this book is available
from the British Library

Published by Ladybird Books Ltd
27 Wrights Lane London W8 5TZ

A Penguin company

© Disney MMI

Based on the Pooh stories by

A.A Milne (copyright The Pooh Properties Trust)

LADYBIRD and the device of a Ladybird are trademarks
of Ladybird Books Ltd

Lost in
the wood

Ladybird

Rabbit

garden

Tigger

Pooh

Piglet

tummy

Rabbit was in the garden.

Along came Tigger.
He bounced on Rabbit.
Rabbit fell down.

Rabbit didn't like being
bounced.
"Stop bouncing, Tigger!"
he said.

Rabbit went to see Piglet
and Pooh.
"Tigger must stop
bouncing," said Rabbit.
"I have a plan."

The next day, Tigger,
Rabbit, Piglet and
Pooh went for a walk
in the wood.

Rabbit, Piglet and Pooh
walked.
Tigger bounced.

Tigger bounced off
into the wood.

"Let's hide," said Rabbit.
"If Tigger gets lost he will
stop bouncing."

Tigger bounced back.
"Where are you?" he said.

Tigger didn't see Rabbit,
Piglet and Pooh.
He bounced off again.
"Let's go home," said Rabbit.

Rabbit and Piglet and Pooh walked into the wood. They walked and walked and walked.

"We are lost," said Piglet.

 17

"We are not lost," said
Rabbit. "Follow me."

So they did. They walked
and walked and walked.

"We are lost," said Pooh.
"We are not lost," said
Rabbit, and he walked
back into the wood.

"I want some honey,"
said Pooh.
"Let's go home,"
said Piglet.

"Yes," said Pooh.
"Let's follow my tummy."
So they did.

On the way they
saw Tigger.
"Rabbit is lost in the wood,"
said Pooh.

"I will find him," said Tigger.
And off he bounced.

Rabbit was scared.

He didn't like the wood.
He didn't like being lost.

Then Rabbit saw Tigger.
"Are you lost, too, Tigger?"
said Rabbit.
"No," said Tigger. "Tiggers
don't get lost."

"Can we go home, now?"
said Rabbit.
"Yes," said Tigger.
"Follow me."

And Rabbit and Tigger
bounced all the way home.